pjbnf

398.45 TROUP

Troupe, Thomas Kingsley, author
Werewolves
33410016724348   11-04-2020

Portage Public Library
2665 Irving Street
Portage, IN 46368

MYTHICAL CREATURES

WEREWOLVES

BY THOMAS KINGSLEY TROUPE

BELLWETHER MEDIA • MINNEAPOLIS, MN

TM

Tórque brims with excitement
perfect for thrill-seekers of all kinds.
Discover daring survival skills, explore
uncharted worlds, and marvel at mighty
engines and extreme sports. In *Torque* books,
anything can happen. Are you ready?

This edition first published in 2021 by Bellwether Media, Inc.

No part of this publication may be reproduced in whole or in part without written
permission of the publisher.
For information regarding permission, write to Bellwether Media, Inc.,
Attention: Permissions Department,
6012 Blue Circle Drive, Minnetonka, MN 55343.

Library of Congress Cataloging-in-Publication Data

Names: Troupe, Thomas Kingsley, author.
Title: Werewolves / by Thomas Kingsley Troupe.
Description: Minneapolis, MN : Bellwether Media, 2021. | Series: Torque |
  Includes bibliographical references and index. | Audience: Ages 7-12 |
  Audience: Grades 4-6 | Summary: "Engaging images accompany information
  about werewolves. The combination of high-interest subject matter and
  light text is intended for students in grades 3 through 7"-Provided by
  publisher.
Identifiers: LCCN 2020014857 (print) | LCCN 2020014858 (ebook) | ISBN
  9781644872796 | ISBN 9781681037424 (ebook)
Subjects: LCSH: Werewolves–Juvenile literature.
Classification: LCC GR830.W4 K56 2021 (print) | LCC GR830.W4 (ebook) |
  DDC 398/.45–dc23
LC record available at https://lccn.loc.gov/2020014857
LC ebook record available at https://lccn.loc.gov/2020014858

Text copyright © 2021 by Bellwether Media, Inc. TORQUE and associated logos are
trademarks and/or registered trademarks of Bellwether Media, Inc.

Editor: Rebecca Sabelko   Designer: Josh Brink

Printed in the United States of America, North Mankato, MN.

TABLE OF CONTENTS

A FULL MOON

Thin clouds float past a full moon. Branches snap nearby. There is something hiding in the woods.

You see yellow eyes watching you through the darkness. The creature snarls and leaps toward you. Run away! It is a werewolf on the hunt!

For centuries, many **cultures** have told tales of werewolves. In some **legends**, people become werewolves after they are bitten by a werewolf. They **transform** into the beasts with each full moon!

Most werewolves look like humans with scary wolf features. Hair covers their faces and bodies. They have big, sharp teeth and long **snouts**. They are hungry and **fierce** beasts.

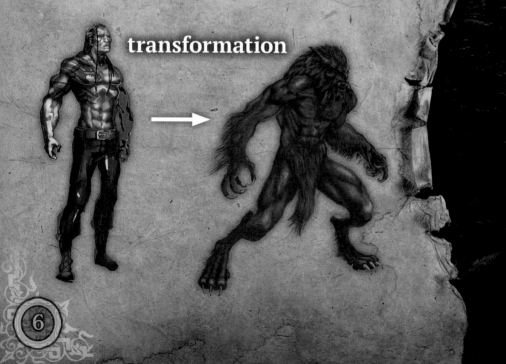

transformation

snout

TRANSFORMATION

It was believed that calling a werewolf by its human name would change it back into its human form.

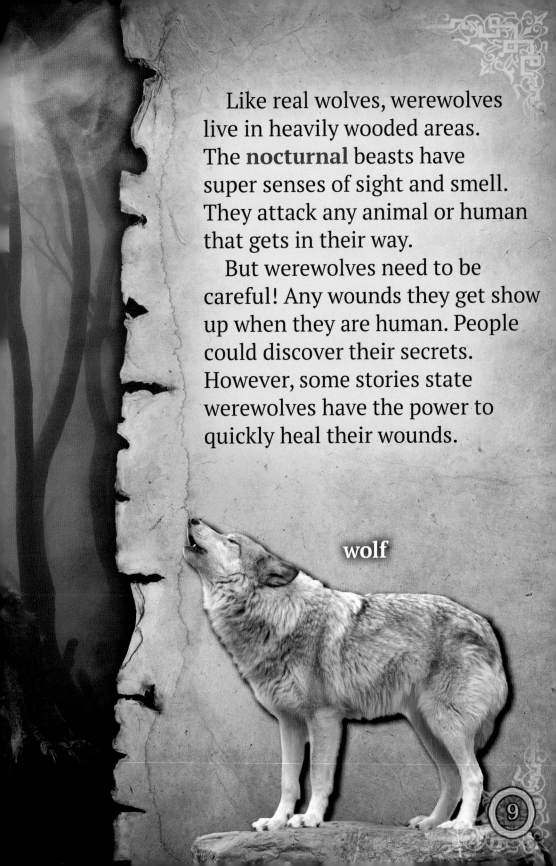

Like real wolves, werewolves
live in heavily wooded areas.
The **nocturnal** beasts have
super senses of sight and smell.
They attack any animal or human
that gets in their way.

But werewolves need to be
careful! Any wounds they get show
up when they are human. People
could discover their secrets.
However, some stories state
werewolves have the power to
quickly heal their wounds.

wolf

WEREWOLF STORIES THROUGH TIME

illustration on a Greek vase

Stories of werewolves come from all around the world. Werewolves first appeared in **literature** between 2100 and 1400 BCE in **Mesopotamia**. In the *Epic of Gilgamesh*, a woman turned a man into a wolf.

Werewolf stories continued around the world. In 425 BCE, Greek historian Herodotus wrote about the Neuri. The Neuri were **nomads** who were believed to transform into wolf shapes. But it is likely the Neuri were simply wearing furs!

Werewolf Origin

Mesopotamia = ☐

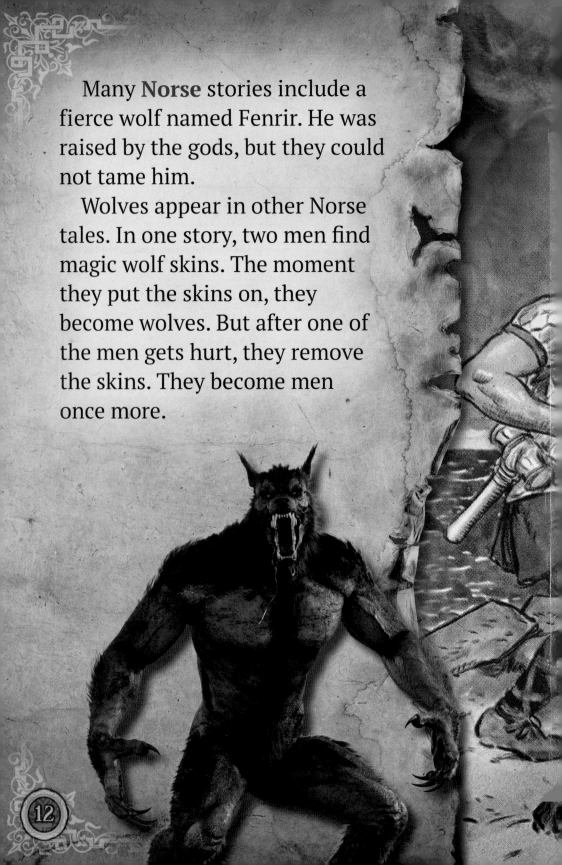

Many **Norse** stories include a fierce wolf named Fenrir. He was raised by the gods, but they could not tame him.

Wolves appear in other Norse tales. In one story, two men find magic wolf skins. The moment they put the skins on, they become wolves. But after one of the men gets hurt, they remove the skins. They become men once more.

UNLUCKY SEVEN

In some South American stories, the seventh son of the seventh son born into a family becomes a werewolf.

Fenrir

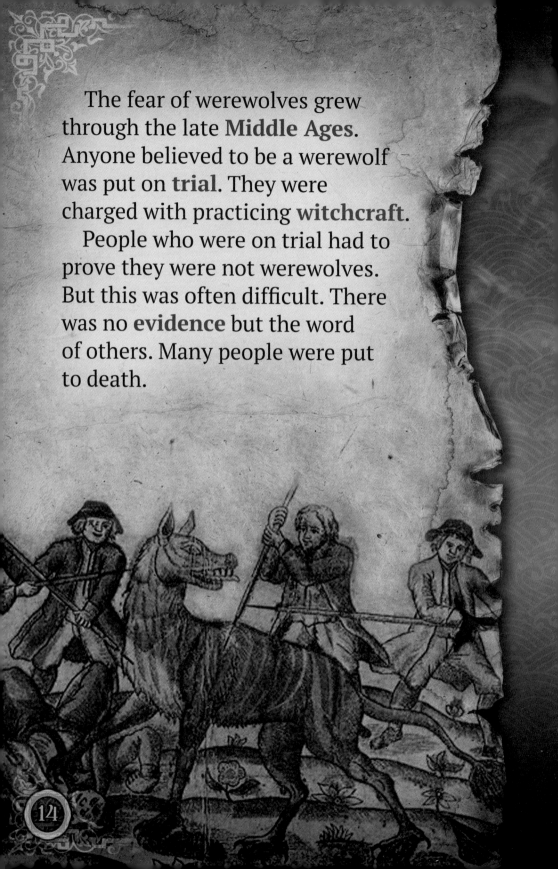

The fear of werewolves grew through the late **Middle Ages**. Anyone believed to be a werewolf was put on **trial**. They were charged with practicing **witchcraft**.

People who were on trial had to prove they were not werewolves. But this was often difficult. There was no **evidence** but the word of others. Many people were put to death.

Shape-shifters Around the World

selkie
(Scotland)

nekomata
(China and Japan)

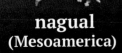

nagual
(Mesoamerica)

naga
(India)

Lack of knowledge led to many werewolf **myths**. People with a lot of hair were often thought to be werewolves.

Other stories are linked to people who live in forests. In 1725, a boy named Peter was found alone in a German forest. Peter ate with his hands and never learned to speak. Many believed he was raised by wolves. This may have led more people to believe in werewolves.

Peter's grave

Werewolf Timeline

Between 2100 and 1400 BCE:
A woman turns a man into a wolf in the *Epic of Gilgamesh*

425 BCE:
Greek historian Herodotus wrote about the Neuri

Between 500 and 1500 CE:
People are put on trial and charged with being werewolves

1725:
A boy named Peter is found in a German forest

WEREWOLVES TODAY

Today, werewolves continue to howl and growl. Many people dress as the hairy monster while they hunt for candy on Halloween.

Werewolves are used to sell products like cell phones and cars. The beasts appear in the world of sports, too. A Canadian baseball team is named the London Werewolves.

werewolf Halloween costume

Movies and video games feature werewolves as well! Sometimes they are shown as helpful and heroic. The Twilight books and films featured a werewolf named Jacob. He befriends the main character, Bella.

The main hero in *The Legend of Zelda: Twilight Princess* video game can turn into a wolf to battle evil. The mythical werewolf continues to be a powerful force in stories around the world!

ALL IN A NAME

The word "lupine" comes from the Latin word for wolf.

Media Mention

Movie: *Harry Potter and the Prisoner of Azkaban*

Year Released: 2004

Description: Remus Lupin, a professor at Hogwarts School of Witchcraft and Wizardry who turns into a werewolf

Skills: uses magic without words or wand, talented in duels, charms, and spells

Harry Potter and the Prisoner of Azkaban

GLOSSARY

cultures—the beliefs, values, and ways of life of groups of people

evidence—something that shows that something else exists or is true

fierce—strong and intense

legends—stories from the past that are believed by many people but cannot be proved to be true

literature—written works, often books, that are highly respected

Mesopotamia—a region of southwestern Asia where many ancient civilizations began

Middle Ages—the period of European history from about 500 to 1500 CE

myths—ancient stories about the beliefs or history of a group of people; myths also try to explain events.

nocturnal—active at night

nomads—people who have no fixed home but wander from place to place

Norse—relating to the people of ancient Norway, Sweden, Denmark, and Iceland

snouts—the noses of some animals

transform—to become something else

trial—the hearing and judgment of something in court

witchcraft—the use of magic

TO LEARN MORE

AT THE LIBRARY

Halls, Kelly Milner. *Cryptid Creatures: A Field Guide*. Seattle, Wash.: Little Bigfoot, 2019.

Lawrence, Sandra, and Stuart Hill. *The Atlas of Monsters: Mythical Creatures from Around the World*. Philadelphia, Pa.: Running Press Kids, 2019.

Pearson, Marie. *Werewolves*. North Mankato, Minn.: Capstone Press, 2020.

ON THE WEB

FACTSURFER

Factsurfer.com gives you a safe, fun way to find more information.

1. Go to www.factsurfer.com

2. Enter "werewolves" into the search box and click 🔍.

3. Select your book cover to see a list of related content.

23

INDEX

The images in this book are reproduced through the courtesy of: andryuha1981, front cover (hero); ehrilif, front cover (background); Denis Simonov, p. 3; DM7, p. 4; Unholy Vault Designs, pp. 4-5; camikuo, p. 6; Enrico Sordi, p. 6 (right); mrjo2405, pp. 6-7; GSoul, pp. 8-9, 12, 23 (werewolf); Allison Coffin, p. 9; Jastrow/ Wiki Commons, p. 10; Album/British Library/ Alamy, pp. 12-13; Keith Corrigan/ Alamy, p. 14; Sawaki Suushi/ Wiki Commons, p. 15 (top left); Jef Thomson, p. 15 (top right); FAMSI.org/ Wiki Commons, p. 15 (bottom left); Ju PhotoStocker, p. 15 (bottom right); David Levenson/ Alamy, p. 16; Free Wind 2014, p. 17 (top); The Picture Art Collection/ Alamy, p. 17 (bottom); Peter Devlin/ Alamy, pp. 18-19; Warner Brothers/ Everett Collection, pp. 20-21; RGR Collection/ Alamy, p. 21; BorisShevchuk, p. 23 (trees).